THE
Stone Bird

For Kieran and Lara, with love —J.M.

For Henry James Hill, and for Freya, my invaluable helper —P.B.

American edition published in 2018 by Andersen Press USA,
an imprint of Andersen Press Ltd.
www.andersenpressusa.com

First published in Great Britain in 2017 by Andersen Press Ltd.,
20 Vauxhall Bridge Road, London SW1V 2SA.

Distributed in the United States and Canada by
Lerner Publishing Group, Inc.
241 First Avenue North
Minneapolis, MN 55401 USA
For reading levels and more information, look up this title at www.lernerbooks.com.

Printed and bound in Malaysia.

Library of Congress Cataloging-in-Publication Data Available
ISBN: 978-1-5415-1455-3
eBook ISBN: 978-1-5415-1469-0
1-TWP-8/1/17

THE
Stone Bird

Jenny McCartney

Patrick Benson

Andersen Press USA

One day in summer, when the sun was blazing hot, Eliza found a stone on the beach. It was smooth, gray, and shaped just like an egg. It fitted inside Eliza's hand perfectly, and she knew that she never wanted to let it go.

When Eliza came home and put it on the
kitchen table, her mother asked,
"Where did you get that stone?"
"It's not a stone," said Eliza firmly. "It's an egg."

"It's much too heavy to be an egg," her mother laughed.
"Well, then," said Eliza, "it's a heavy egg."
And she went upstairs and hid it underneath her pillow.

At bedtime, when the air was too hot in her
room, she liked to take the stone out and feel its
coolness against her cheek and the weight of it
in her hand. It was her stony secret.

But one night, when she pressed it close to her
face, the stone felt very warm. So she put it on
her bedside table instead and fell asleep.

Eliza was awoken by the sound of something cracking. There, on her bedside table, sat a stone bird.

She blinked in case she was dreaming, but it was still there—gray all over, with a pointy beak and little eyes that looked as if they knew something.

The stone bird never moved, not even a tiny
bit, but Eliza loved it. She slipped it into her
pocket and set it next to her plate at mealtimes.
Wherever she went, her stone bird went too.

Her mother said, "Where did you get that thing?"
"It's not a thing," said Eliza. "It's a bird."
Her mother smiled, "It's too hard to be a bird."
"Well, then," said Eliza, "it's a hard bird."

Fall came, and the golden leaves crackled like paper under
Eliza's new school shoes. Now that she was busy
at school, the bird never left her bedside table.

One morning, she suddenly saw something
lying next to it. A small, gray, oval stone.
"Where did you pick up that pebble?" her mother asked.
"It's not a pebble," said Eliza quietly. "It's a little egg."
This time, her mother said nothing.
She just stroked Eliza's hair.

Soon it was winter, and frost laced the corners
of Eliza's bedroom window. At night she was warm
beneath her feather quilt, but she worried that
the stone bird and its egg would freeze.

So she made them a nest from a pair of socks and whispered,
"Don't worry. It will be spring soon."

On Christmas Day, Eliza
rolled a crumb of cake
beneath the bird's beak.
But later, as she played
with her new dolls and
trucks and puzzles, she
hardly thought about
the stone bird or her
egg at all.

By the time spring came, Eliza had grown tired of
waiting. Maybe the little egg really was just a pebble.

Then one day, when the trees were in bud,
she heard a tiny cracking sound from her bedside
table. She turned around quickly and saw that, next
to her stone bird, was a second, much smaller one.

Eliza felt as if she would burst with excitement.
"You did it!" she whispered to the stone bird.
"You hatched a chick." It didn't move, but Eliza
thought that something in its eyes looked happy.

When the weather got warmer, Eliza's mother opened the
window in her room to let the breeze in.
That night, Eliza dreamed she
heard the beating of wings.

When she woke up,
the sock nest was empty.
Her birds had gone. She
hunted under the bed
and behind the curtains.
She rummaged through
all her dresser drawers.

"Did you move my birds?"
she shouted to her mother.
"I never touch your stones,
except when I'm tidying up,"
her mother called back calmly.

"They're not stones," Eliza
muttered furiously. "They're
birds." And she lay down on
her bed and cried.

Eliza thought about her birds every day,
wondering where they were. Her mother offered
to take her to the beach and get more stones.

"I don't want stones. I want my birds back,"
Eliza told her angrily. Not even the idea
of her birthday made her smile.

On her birthday morning, when everyone else was still asleep, Eliza was awoken by a sharp little *rat-tat-tat* at her windowpane, like the pecking of a beak.

She jumped out of bed and raced over to the window, but there was nothing there.

Then, over on the roof of the garden shed, she saw two gray birds looking up toward her window.

The first bird spread its wings and flew toward her, almost brushing the glass with its wing tips before it soared into the sky.

Then the second one joined it, and together they circled higher and higher until they disappeared.

Eliza looked down and saw a big, soft, gray feather trembling on the windowsill, gleaming like silver in the morning sunlight.

When her mother saw the feather in Eliza's hand, she said, "That's beautiful. Where did you get it?"

"It's a present," said Eliza. "From my birds."